Tyra
the Designer
Fairy

To Isabella with love

Special thanks to Rachel Elliot

No part of this publication may be reproduced, stored in a retrieval system, or transmitted in any form or by any means, electronic, mechanical, photocopying, recording, or otherwise, without written permission of the publisher. For information regarding permission, write to Rainbow Magic Limited c/o HIT Entertainment, 830 South Greenville Avenue, Allen, TX 75002-3320.

ISBN 978-0-545-48486-2

12 11 10 9 8 7 6 5 4 3 2 1   13 14 15 16 17 18/0

Printed in China   68

This edition first printing, July 2013

Tyra the Designer Fairy

by Daisy Meadows

SCHOLASTIC INC.

The
Fairyland
Palace

Tippington
Fountains
SHOPPING CENTER

Fashion Show

Top Hats & Tiaras

FASHION

HARTLEYS

Ice Blue
Hair Salon

TIPPINGTON TOYS

Ice Blue
booth

I'm the king of designer fashion,
Looking stylish is my passion.
Ice Blue's the name of my fashion line,
The designs are fabulous and they're all mine!

Some people think my clothes are odd,
But I will get the fashion world's nod.
Fashion Fairy magic will make my dream come true —
Soon everyone will wear Ice Blue!

Contents

Funny Fashions

"I can't wait for the design competition workshop to start," said Kirsty Tate, peeking into her bag with excitement. "I have my colorful scarves, and I'm going to sew them into a flowing dress."

"It will be great!" said her best friend, Rachel Walker. "I'm going to paint a glittery rainbow on my old jeans."

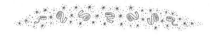

"And I'm going to have lunch with my friend Moira," said Mrs. Walker. "So we're all in store for a fun day!"

They were standing inside the new Tippington Fountains Shopping Center. Kirsty was staying with Rachel for the school break, and they had been having a very exciting time ever since the new mall had opened. A design competition had been announced on the opening day, and the girls had been working on their ideas ever since. After the workshop, all the kids' creations would be judged, and the winners would model their clothes in a charity fashion show at the end of the week.

"Let's go this way," said Mrs. Walker. "I told Moira I'd meet her outside the wedding-dress shop, Top Hats & Tiaras."

They walked along slowly, looking from one side to the other at all the exciting stores. Then Rachel nudged Kirsty. "Look at that lady over there," she said. "She's wearing one pant leg long and the other one is short."

"And her son only has one sock on," said Kirsty. "That's strange."

"New fashions always seem strange at first," said Mrs. Walker

with a laugh. "Look, there's Moira over there, and she has safety pins on her cardigan instead of buttons. What will the fashion designers think of next?"

As Mrs. Walker went to give Moira a

hug, Kirsty and Rachel exchanged a glance. "These aren't funny new fashions," said Rachel. "It's Jack Frost and his goblins causing trouble!"

At the beginning of the week, Kirsty and Rachel had gone to a Fairyland fashion

show, but Jack Frost and his goblins had barged in. Jack Frost had created his own designer label named Ice Blue, and he and the goblins were wearing the new designs. He wanted everyone in the human world and Fairyland to wear his clothes, so they would all look just like him!

With a bolt of icy magic, Jack had stolen the Fashion Fairies' magical objects and brought them to Tippington Fountains Shopping Center. The fairies needed their magical objects to take care of every aspect of fashion — in both the human world and in Fairyland. Now everything was going wrong in both fashion worlds!

"I'll see you at the competition later," called Mrs. Walker. "Have fun, girls!"

Kirsty and
Rachel waved
good-bye.

"We still have
half an hour
before the
workshop starts,"
said Rachel. "Let's
go and see if we can find any goblins."

The worried Fashion Fairies had
asked for the girls' help. Of course
Kirsty and Rachel had said yes! They
had already helped two of the fairies
find their magic objects. But Jack Frost
and his goblins were becoming cleverer
and even trickier. Would the girls be
able to find the other objects in time
to save the fashion show at the end of
the week?

Rachel and Kirsty started their search
for goblins in Hartley's Department
Store.

"Don't forget to look under shelves and
behind the sales racks," said Kirsty.
"Goblins can hide in really tiny spaces.
They could be anywhere."

Rachel started to check a rack of shirts,
while Kirsty got down on her knees and
looked under
a low shelf.

"Look at
this," said
Rachel,
holding up a
blouse that
was full of big
holes. "What a
fashion disaster!"

Kirsty shook her head sadly and stood up, but then she immediately tripped.

"Are you all right?" asked Rachel, hurrying over to help her friend.

"I'm fine," said Kirsty. "But what did I trip on?" They looked down and saw a pair of pants dragging on the ground from a clothing rack.

"Those pant legs are way too long," said Rachel. "We have to find the goblins and stop them!"

Everywhere the girls looked in the

store, they found clothes that were misshaped, ripped, or stained. They stopped beside a display of fall fashions and Kirsty groaned.

"Look at that!" she exclaimed.

The mannequin in the middle of the display had a tear in the back of her jeans! The girls looked at the others in the display, checking to see if their clothes were ruined, too. As Rachel examined a mannequin in a long bronze dress, she noticed something strange.

"That dress looks like it's glowing," she said. "Down by the right-hand pocket — can you see it, Kirsty?"

"Yes!" said Kirsty, moving closer. "It looks like . . . magic!"

A Worrying Workshop

There was a fizz of sparkling fairy dust, and then Tyra the Designer Fairy climbed out of the dress pocket!

"Hello, Tyra!" said the girls with excitement.

Tyra looked cool in her ruffled skirt and funky leopard-print suspenders, but her dark eyes were worried.

"Hi, Kirsty!" she replied. "Hi, Rachel.
I'm here to try and get my magical tape
measure back from Jack Frost and the
goblins. Everywhere I go I see awful-
looking clothes that don't fit well, and
it's making me really sad that I can't do
my job!"

"We've seen some strange fashions,
too," said Kirsty. "Don't worry, Tyra.
We'll help you. We've already been
looking for goblins this morning."

"Did you find any?" Tyra asked.

"Not yet," said Rachel. "Let's keep
searching."

"But we have to go to the workshop,"
said Kirsty, looking at her watch. "It's
about to start!"

"What about Tyra?" asked Rachel.

"No problem," said Tyra, zooming into

Kirsty's bag of scarves. "I'll hide in here. Fabulous colors, Kirsty!"

The girls hurried to the magnificent fountain area in the middle of the shopping mall. It was crowded with girls and boys, all sitting at long tables. The tables were piled high with ribbons, sequins, and colorful materials in lots of different textures and sizes.

"Look, there's Jessica Jarvis!" said Rachel when she noticed the supermodel who was helping to organize the competition.

"And there's Ella McCauley," Kirsty added, spotting the famous designer.

The two celebrities were setting up the last table for the workshop. As Rachel and Kirsty moved toward two empty chairs, they saw Ella look down at her

 arms in surprise. "Oh my goodness, this jacket has one sleeve that's longer than the other!" she exclaimed. "How did I miss that? How embarrassing!"

"No one will notice if you roll them both up," said Jessica. "Look at what I did — I'm wearing two different-colored shoes!"

Rachel and Kirsty took their places at one of the tables with some other girls and boys. Everyone was talking eagerly, and no one seemed to notice the strange fashion mistakes that the celebrities had made.

"I don't see any goblins lurking around," said Rachel in a low voice. "I hope they stay away from the workshop!"

Tyra peeked over the top of Kirsty's bag.

"I'm worried about the workshop," she said, frowning. "If Jessica and Ella are having fashion disasters, anything could happen!"

At that moment, Ella clapped her hands together and the chatting girls and boys fell silent.

"Hi, everyone," said Ella. "It's great that so many of you have shown up for the workshop. Some of you already know that I'm a fashion designer, and that makes me very lucky. I get to do something that I love every day!"

Her eyes were sparkling with excitement. Rachel noticed that she had rolled up her sleeves.

"When I'm designing a new dress, I start by drawing it on paper," Ella explained. "Then I choose the fabric I want to use, and measure it carefully. Finally, I sew the pieces together to make the dress."

It sounded wonderful, and Kirsty felt her fingers itching to get started.

"I'd like you all to meet Mabel," said Ella.

She brought out a life-size dressmaker's mannequin, which was purple. There was a dial on Mabel's back that  looked a little like the face of a watch. There were numbers printed around the edge.

"By turning this dial, I can change Mabel's dress size," Ella continued. "It means that I can design clothes for people of all different shapes and sizes."

Ella handed out some of her designs so everyone could see how to start designing.

"You can find paper and pencils on the tables," she announced. "Start planning your designs, and I will walk around and help anyone who needs advice."

Kirsty and Rachel picked up their pencils and started to sketch. They had imagined their outfits so many times that it was easy to draw every detail.

"I love your dress," said Rachel, looking at Kirsty's drawing.

"I'd buy your jeans if I saw them in a store," Kirsty replied with a grin.

"Me, too," said a voice behind them.

They looked around and saw Ella looking over their shoulders. She smiled at them.

"I think both of your designs are fantastic," she said. "Let me help you

measure the scarves and jeans you're using." She took out a tape measure and stretched it along Rachel's jeans. Then she took out a small white pencil.

"This is a dressmaking pencil," she said. "I use it to mark measurements on clothes without damaging them."

She leaned forward and then paused.

"I don't believe it!" she exclaimed.

Goblins in Blue

"Look at the numbers on this tape measure," said Ella. "They're all messed up!"

Rachel and Kirsty looked down. Sure enough, the numbers were all in the wrong order.

"That's because Tyra's magic tape measure is missing," whispered Kirsty.

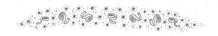

"What are we going to do without a tape measure?" asked Rachel, worried that she wouldn't be able to finish her design.

"Don't panic," said Ella. "I have a few tricks up my sleeve!" She winked at them and pulled a ball of string out of her pocket. "You can mark the measurements using a length of string," she said. "It'll work just as well."

As Ella moved away, Tyra looked up at the girls.

"I'm going to go and see if I can spot the goblins while you finish your clothes," she said. "There's a beautiful flower basket hanging from the railing  on the second floor, and it overlooks the fountain area. I'll be able to see any goblins from up there — and keep an eye on you, too!"

The girls started making their outfits while Tyra fluttered up to the flower basket, being careful not to be seen.

Rachel concentrated on drawing the rainbow on her jeans with glitter paint, while Kirsty started to sew her scarves together.

After a few minutes, the girls heard a groan from the table next to them. They saw a boy holding up a shirt that was a few sizes too big. Rachel looked down at her jeans.

"Oh, no!" she exclaimed. "Look, Kirsty — my rainbow stripes are all crooked."

Kirsty put her arm around her friend's shoulder.

"I'll help you fix them," she said in a comforting voice. "I'll just go and try on my scarf dress, and then we can repaint the stripes together."

She carefully picked up her dress and took it to the curtained-off dressing room in the corner. A few minutes later she came out, swishing the dress around and smiling.

"That looks wonderful!" cried Rachel.

Kirsty stood in front of the mirror and looked carefully at her creation. Then her smile faded.

"The hem is lopsided!" She groaned. "Look, Rachel — it's longer on the left than on the right. And I thought I measured so carefully!"

Kirsty changed back into her ordinary clothes. When she came out of the dressing room, Rachel motioned to her and put her finger to her lips.

"Do you hear something?" she whispered.

Kirsty strained her ears. Over the
chatter of the other girls and boys, she
could hear a faint voice like the far-off
ringing of bells.

"Kirsty! Rachel!"

"It's Tyra!" the girls said together.

They looked up
and saw Tyra
leaning out of
the flower
basket. She
was beckoning
to them. She
had her wand
pressed to her
throat.

"She must be using
magic so we can hear her,"
said Kirsty.

"She's pointing at something over there," Rachel said. "What did she see?"

Tyra was pointing to a group of four boys arriving at one of the workshop tables. They were all wearing bright blue outfits with high shoulders and tight pants.

"Look at their enormous shoes!" said Kirsty. "They're goblins, I'm sure of it!"

"That must be why Tyra was pointing at them," Rachel agreed. "Come on, let's get closer. We have to find out what they're up to!"

The goblins' table was piled high with fabric in many different shades of blue. Beside it was a dressmaker's mannequin on wheels. But this mannequin was nothing like Mabel. It was tall and blue. When one of the goblins spun it around, Kirsty gasped. It looked exactly like Jack Frost!

Suddenly, Kirsty felt something tickle the back of her neck. Tyra had flown down and hidden herself behind a lock of Kirsty's hair.

"Can you and Rachel go somewhere private?" said Tyra quietly. "I think we'll have a better chance of finding the magic tape measure if I change you into fairies."

Kirsty touched Rachel's arm.

"Tyra wants to turn us into fairies," she said in a low voice. "Let's hide in the fitting room."

They told Ella that they were going to get something that would help them with their designs, and then they hurried into the dressing room. Tyra fluttered out and waved her wand over the girls. Their skin tingled as a puff of rainbow-colored

fairy dust billowed
around them and
glittery wings
unfurled from
their shoulders.
In no time, the
girls were
fairy-size.

The three
fairies fluttered out
of the dressing room and
made their way toward the goblins'
table. They flitted between baskets of
material, being very careful to stay out
of sight.

"Let's hide in here," said Rachel,
slipping under a large pile of blue fabric.
"Now we'll be able to hear everything
the goblins say."

Shopping-center Chaos

The goblins were chatting and giggling.
They sounded very proud of themselves.

"Does anyone need any help?" asked
Jessica, who was just walking past the
table.

"Not from you!" said the rude goblins.

Jessica looked surprised, but walked
away.

"Jack Frost is going to love this outfit," said a short goblin with a long nose. "He has to reward us for this."

"I think he'll like my part the best," said another goblin, who had a blue scarf wrapped around his waist like a belt.

"No way," sneered a third goblin, who had a blue top hat balanced on his bony head. "Mine's better than yours."

"Each goblin is making a different section of the outfit," Kirsty realized. "Look — that goblin has the collar, and that one has a pant leg."

"What a funny way to make an outfit," said Tyra, frowning.

"Give me that tape measure," demanded a skinny goblin with a pimple on the tip of his nose.

"What's the magic word?" demanded the goblin with the scarf.

"NOW!" yelled the skinny goblin.

There was a little scuffle and then the skinny goblin grabbed a shiny golden tape measure from the other's hand. Tyra gasped.

"That's my magic tape measure!" she said, clasping Rachel's arm in excitement. "We found it!"

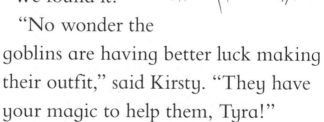

"No wonder the goblins are having better luck making their outfit," said Kirsty. "They have your magic to help them, Tyra!"

"That's it!" announced the skinny goblin. "I'm finished. Let's put the outfit together."

The goblins scrambled over to the mannequin and started to dress it, sewing the pieces of the outfit together as they worked.

"They left the magic tape measure on the table," said Kirsty. "Now's our chance to grab it!"

The three fairies edged closer to the golden tape measure. They stayed close to the piles of fabric in case they needed to hide quickly. The goblins finished putting the outfit together and stepped back to admire it.

"It's a work of art!" said the skinny goblin.

"Jack Frost will love it," declared the long-nosed goblin.

"They're not looking!" whispered Tyra. "Now's our chance!"

Kirsty reached out her hand and touched the edge of the tape measure. She started to pull it toward her, but just then the long-nosed goblin gave a loud yelp.

"It's my turn to carry the tape measure now!" he said, grabbing at it. "You guys have been hogging it all day."

"No way!" shouted the goblin in the top hat. "It's my turn!"

"Mine!" yelled the other two goblins.

The long-nosed goblin stuck out his tongue at them and then raced off through the mall.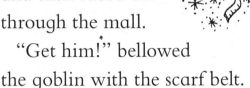

"Get him!" bellowed the goblin with the scarf belt.

They all ran after him, and the three fairies joined in the chase, flying close to the high ceiling so that they wouldn't be seen.

The long-nosed goblin was a fast runner, and he led the others around the shopping mall at top speed, not caring who he bumped into along the way.

Their shouts and squeals made everyone
stare at them.

"Oh, those awful goblins!" said Tyra.
"They're causing so much trouble!"

Rachel and Kirsty couldn't reply —
they needed all their energy to fly as fast
as they could!

The rowdy goblins hurtled into Top Hats & Tiaras, where the goblin with the scarf belt skidded into a long rack of wedding dresses and came out wrapped in ivory silk. The others pointed at him and laughed as loud as they could.

"You naughty kids!" cried the shop manager. "Get out of here at once!"

As the goblins scurried out, Rachel and Kirsty noticed a bride coming out of the shop's fitting room. Tears welled up in her eyes, and there was a big pink stain down the front of her dress.

"It's ruined," she was saying. "What am I going to do?"

The girls felt very sorry for her, but there was no time to stop and help. They zoomed after the goblins, who had disappeared into the Comfy Feet shoe store. Shoes flew up into the air as the goblins charged through the aisles. The store was in chaos. Customers were waving shoes and yelling. The store manager was pulling his hair and shouting into the phone. "I'm telling you, there isn't

a single pair of matching shoes in the entire store!" he said. "I have tons of angry customers here."

The girls swooped over his head and chased the goblins into the stockroom at the back of the store. The goblin in the top hat had been distracted by all the shoes and was busy trying on a purple boot and a green-spotted clog. But the others had disappeared!

Mannequin Mischief

"Look — there's a door at the back of the room," said Kirsty.

"But it's closing!" Tyra cried in alarm. "Quick, girls!"

The three fairies zipped toward the exit, and whisked through with only an inch to spare. Rachel felt the door brush against her wings as it shut tight.

"That was close!" she said.

They found themselves back at the fountain, on the other side of the workshop. The three remaining goblins were running around the fountain so quickly that they looked like blue blurs.

"How can we stop them?" asked Tyra.

Rachel looked around. Nearby was the Sweet Scoop Ice Cream Parlor with a tray of free samples outside.

"I have an idea," she said. "Tyra, can you use your magic to turn all the ice-cream samples blue? If we can distract the goblins, we might be able to get the magic tape measure back."

Tyra nodded and sent a stream of rainbow-colored sparkles over to the tray. Instantly, the ice cream turned ice blue. A few seconds later, the goblin with the scarf belt sped over to the tray.

"Ice cream! Yum!" he exclaimed. "It's the same color as the Ice Blue clothes! I've got to try it!"

The skinny goblin joined him, and soon they were both wolfing down the delicious ice cream.

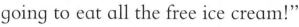

"They're so greedy," said Tyra. "They're going to eat all the free ice cream!"

"But where's the goblin with the tape measure?" asked Rachel.

"Over there!" Kirsty exclaimed, pointing.

Instead of gobbling up the blue ice cream with the others, the long-nosed goblin was scurrying back to the workshop with the magic tape measure.

"He must want to finish Jack Frost's outfit," Tyra said. The fairies sighed with disappointment. "How are we going to

get the
magic tape
measure
back now?"

Kirsty
watched as
the goblin
added some
final stitches
to the outfit.
He looked very
happy with
himself, and that
gave her an idea.

"I have a plan," she said. "Tyra, can
you turn us back to our human size
again, please? If we flatter the goblin,
maybe we can distract him from the
tape measure."

The girls hid
behind a giant
flowerpot next to
the fountain, and
Tyra waved her
wand again.
Instantly, Rachel
and Kirsty were
transformed back to

their normal size. Tyra tucked herself
under Kirsty's hair, and they walked over
to where the goblin was putting the
finishing touches on the outfit.

"What a wonderful creation!" said
Kirsty in a loud voice.

"Whoever designed this must be very
talented," said Rachel.

The long-nosed goblin puffed out
his chest.

"That was me,"
he said proudly.

"Wow, that's
impressive," said
Rachel. "Is it
for you?"

The goblin shook
his head.

"That's too bad,"

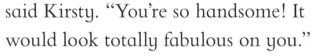

said Kirsty. "You're so handsome! It
would look totally fabulous on you."

"You're right," said the goblin with
a sigh.

"You could always resize it, so it will
fit you," Rachel remarked in a soft voice.

The goblin stared at Rachel, his hands
slowly reaching for the outfit. Then he
excitedly started to trim it down to
his size.

"Would you like me to measure it for you?" asked Rachel, looking hopefully at the tape measure.

"No, that's mine," the goblin snapped.

He held on to it tightly, even when he took the outfit into the dressing room to get changed. As soon as the curtain closed, Rachel turned to Kirsty in alarm.

"What are we going to do now?" she whispered.

"Quick, help me move the mannequin over to the dressing room," said Kirsty.

The Jack Frost mannequin moved easily and quietly on its wheels.

"Tyra, can you make yourself sound like Jack Frost?" asked Kirsty in a low voice. "If the goblin believes the real Jack Frost is here, he might hand over the tape measure."

Tyra waved her wand, but then the dressing room curtain swished open and the goblin came out.

"Too soon!" exclaimed Kirsty.

She gave the mannequin a push and sent it skidding toward the goblin.

"Give me the magic tape measure, you fool," said Tyra in Jack Frost's voice.

The goblin froze, and his eyes nearly popped out of his head. All he could see was Jack Frost speeding toward him.

"Help!" he squeaked.

He threw the magic tape measure into the air and started running. As the mannequin crashed into the dressing room, Tyra caught the magic tape measure in her outstretched hand. It immediately shrank to fairy-size.

"I got it!" she cheered.

Rachel and Kirsty burst into squeals of laughter. Tyra was still talking in Jack Frost's voice!

The girls hurried back to the design competition workshop. Most of the boys and girls had finished their outfits.

"Five more minutes," Jessica announced.

"Oh, no!" cried Rachel. "We're not going to have time to fix our outfits!"

A Surprise Competitor!

"I'm not going to let that happen," said Tyra, who was hiding underneath Kirsty's hair. "You would have had time if you hadn't been helping me, so it's only fair that I help you now."

She gave her wand a little flick, and the perfect scarf appeared beside the hem

of Kirsty's dress. Some tubes of fabric
paint appeared next to Rachel's jeans.

Quickly, the girls got to work. They
fixed the problems as fast as they could.
Rachel had just painted the final stripe
on her rainbow when Jessica clapped her
hands together.

"Time's up!" she announced. "Thank
you all for working so hard. It's time to
get ready for the competition!"

"All the other outfits look amazing,"
said Kirsty, gazing around.

"Thanks to you," said Tyra, using her
magic to quickly dry Rachel's jeans. "They
would have been fashion disasters if you
hadn't helped me get my tape measure
back. How can I ever thank you enough?"

"You already have," said Rachel,
patting her jeans. "It's been fun!"

"I have to take the tape measure back to Fairyland now," said Tyra. "Good-bye, Rachel and Kirsty! Good luck in the competition!"

She zoomed high above the fountain, gave the girls a final wave, and disappeared in a puff of rainbow-colored fairy dust.

The shopping mall was getting very busy. Lots of people were arriving to watch the competition. They gathered around the fountain as everyone changed into their new fashions. Kirsty's brightly colored dress swirled around her ankles, and the paint on Rachel's jeans sparkled in the lights. They felt very proud of their hard work.

"Look, there's your mom in the crowd," said Kirsty.

They waved to Mrs. Walker and her friend Moira, who was standing beside her. A small stage had been built next to the fountain, and all the contestants walked onto it and stood in a row. Rachel and Kirsty squeezed each other's hands.

Jessica and Ella walked onto the stage with a short man in a dark gray suit.

"Ladies and gentlemen, boys and girls, welcome to the competition," said Jessica with a beaming smile. "The contestants have been working hard on their designs, and now it's our job to choose which ones will participate in the fashion show."

Ella stepped forward. "Jessica and I will be judging the competition with the manager of Hartley's Department Store, Owen Jacobs. Please be patient while we make our decisions."

The three judges started to walk along the line. They examined each design closely and carefully. But they had only looked at a couple of entries when there

was a scuffle in the crowd. A late entrant
ran onto the stage! He had spiky hair
and a nasty scowl.

"It's Jack Frost!" cried Rachel.

Jack Frost elbowed his way into the line.
He was wearing the outfit that the goblins
had made, but it was much too small for
him. When the judges reached him, they
all exchanged surprised glances.

"Um, well, it's a good try," said Owen.
"But it's a little on the
small side."

Jack Frost
narrowed his eyes.

"You need
to practice
measuring,"
Jessica said
kindly.

Jack Frost curled his lip.

"Maybe it would look better on one of your little friends, who we met earlier?" Ella suggested.

When he heard this, Jack Frost looked like steam might come out of his ears!

"You don't know what you're talking about!" he roared. "I'll show you what real fashion is! Just you wait and see!"

As he turned and stormed off the platform, there was a loud ripping sound, and a split tore up the back of his pants.

"I wonder what he meant by that," Kirsty said quietly.

But there was no time for Rachel to reply. The judges were now in front of them! The girls held their breaths as Jessica, Ella, and Owen walked around them, looking at their outfits.

"These are great outfits," said Owen. "I especially like the creative flair of the scarf dress!"

"The detail in your rainbow is wonderful," Ella told Rachel with a smile.

"We'd love you to model your outfits in the fashion show at the end of the week," said Jessica. "Nice work, both of you!"

The girls were thrilled, and they gave each other a big hug. In the crowd, Mrs. Walker was smiling and clapping.

"I'm so excited!" whispered Rachel as the judges moved on. "I just hope that we can stop Jack Frost before the fashion

show. There are still four magic objects
to find."

"Of course we can," said Kirsty firmly.
"The fairies are depending on us, and
we're not going to let them down!"

Kirsty and Rachel have helped
Tyra find her measuring tape.
Now it's time for them to help

Alexa
the Fashion Reporter Fairy!

Read on for a sneak peek. . . .

Fashion Magic

"What should we call our fashion magazine, Rachel?" Kirsty asked, tapping her pencil thoughtfully on her sketch pad. "I can't think of a good title!"

The girls were in the beautiful landscaped park that surrounded the new Tippington Fountains Shopping Center, an enormous building of chrome and glass. Kirsty had come to stay with Rachel for the school break, and Mrs. Walker had taken them to the grand opening of Tippington Fountains earlier that week. Yesterday, Rachel and Kirsty had attended a workshop for the design competition at the shopping mall. The girls had enjoyed it so much, they'd decided to create their own fashion magazine! They were sitting on a picnic blanket on a soft carpet of red, yellow, and orange autumn leaves with their sketch pads and colored pencils.

Rachel was finishing a design for a T-shirt. "I'm not sure," she replied, glancing up as more leaves drifted down from the trees above them. "*Fashion for Girls*?"

"How about *Fantastic Fashions*?"

suggested Rachel's dad. He was sitting nearby on a park bench, reading a newspaper.

"*Fabulous Fashions?*" Kirsty said, then shook her head. "No, that's not special enough. What about *Fashion Magic?*"

"Perfect!" Rachel said with a grin. She held up her sketch pad to show Kirsty her T-shirt design. The T-shirt was bright orange with TIPPINGTON FOUNTAINS written in gold and red letters across the front. Below the words, Rachel had added a drawing of the spectacular fountains in the middle of the shopping mall.

RAINBOW magic™

There's Magic in Every Series!

The Rainbow Fairies
The Weather Fairies
The Jewel Fairies
The Pet Fairies
The Fun Day Fairies
The Petal Fairies
The Dance Fairies
The Music Fairies
The Sports Fairies
The Party Fairies
The Ocean Fairies
The Night Fairies
The Magical Animal Fairies
The Princess Fairies
The Superstar Fairies

Read them all!

📖 **SCHOLASTIC**

scholastic.com
rainbowmagiconline.com

HiT entertainment

RMFA